Alicia!

Congratulations on tenure! Enjoy this book as I know you love mangoes, probably more than I do. I've enjoyed the richness of our friendship.

Love,
Susan

A Season for Mangoes

by **Regina Hanson**

Illustrated by **Eric Velasquez**

Clarion Books / New York

The author thanks George and Ruth Turner and Veronica James
for background information on Jamaican culture.
Special thanks to Michele Coppola and Dinah Stevenson.

Clarion Books
a Houghton Mifflin Company imprint
215 Park Avenue South, New York, NY 10003

The illustrations were executed in oil paint on Fabriano watercolor paper.
The text was set in 16-point OPTIPowell-Oldstyle.

www.houghtonmifflinbooks.com

Printed in Singapore

Library of Congress Cataloging-in-Publication Data

Hanson, Regina.
A season for mangoes / by Regina Hanson ; illustrated by Eric Velasquez.
p. cm.
Summary: In Jamaica, Sareen is concerned about participating in her first sit-up, a celebration of
the life of her recently deceased grandmother, but discovers that sharing her stories
of Nana's passion for mangoes helps lift the sadness.
ISBN 0-618-15972-X
[1. Stage fright—Fiction. 2. Funeral rites and ceremonies—Fiction. 3. Grandmothers—Fiction.
4. Storytelling—Fiction. 5. Jamaica—Fiction.] I. Velasquez, Eric, ill. II. Title.
PZ7.H1989Se 2004
[E]—dc22
2003025972

ISBN-13: 978-0-618-15972-7

ISBN-10: 0-618-15972-X

TWP 10 9 8 7 6 5 4 3 2 1

To Bill, Alexander, Alfred-Albert, Adam, and Rich
—R.H.

For my mother, Carmen Lydia:
thanks for the paintbrushes
—E.V.

"Don't be scared, Sareen. It'll be all right," my twin brother, Desmond, whispers to me.

I grip his hand as we settle onto one of the many benches in the yard.

Lanterns hang from our huge mango tree like shining fruit. Our home and yard wear necklaces of lights, and oil lamps set the air aglow.

The whole village is here. Sweat trickles down my back as I imagine myself talking in front of so many people.

It is the night of my first sit-up. In my village in Jamaica, a sit-up celebrates the life of a loved one who has recently died. Tonight we'll celebrate my grandmother, my beloved Nana.

I really want to tell my stories about Nana, but I'm also afraid I'll burst into tears.

5

The leader of the sit-up is Maas Halroy. He begins
by singing a hymn, and we all join in. Then one by one
people tell their stories of Nana.

Miss Velma goes first. She says, "One morning I saw Nana hiding behind her hibiscus bushes. Some schoolchildren walked up. One said, 'Look at all these shoe-flowers. Let's polish our shoes!'

"The children picked some red hibiscus flowers. As they began to rub their dark shoes with them, Nana jumped out from behind the bushes. 'I caught you!' she shouted. You should have heard her laugh as the children squealed!

"Then Nana helped them pick more shoe-flowers, and she lent them a buffing rag. She got kisses, and they went to school with stained fingers and glossy shoes."

We all cheer Miss Velma's story, the children loudest of all.

Between the stories, everyone samples the food that friends cooked in our yard all day. Desmond and I get curried goat and boiled green bananas. While enjoying the peppery seasonings in the gravy, I think about my stories of Nana. Before the sit-up, Maas Halroy told me that they are special, best saved for later. But suppose, when I open my mouth to speak, no sound comes?

My hunger vanishes as my stomach plays leapfrog with itself.
A conch shell horn sounds. Maas Halroy says, "Because we
will always love Nana, in our hearts she is always alive. So let's
entertain her!"

People tell humorous tales about Anancy, the mischievous spider man.
He moved to Jamaica with some of our long-ago ancestors, to cheer them
up after they were brought here from West Africa as slaves.

Next come the big lies. Desmond says, "Yesterday I saw a mosquito riding a bicycle. He rode the hundred miles to Kingston so fast that when he got there, it was an hour earlier than when he left home!"

My brother speaks so well. Now the idea of telling my stories makes me shiver. I don't think I'll be able to.

Maas Halroy says, "Ring games!"
Desmond and I sit with our friends in a circle
on the ground. Each of us hits the ground with a
stone, marking the beat of our song. Then each of
us passes the stone to the friend on the right, all
in rhythm.

Go down to Manuel Road, girl and boy,
to go break rock-stone.
Break them one by one, girl and boy,
break them two by two.
Mash your finger? Don't cry, girl and boy,
for it's only a game. . . .

14

Our game makes me remember our ancestors, who had to smash rocks and build winding roads through the mountains. Afterward, as we sweeten our chocolate tea with unrefined sugar, I think of their hard labor on sugar cane plantations.

15

When Maas Halroy glances at me, my palms turn cold.

"I'm not ready," I whisper to Desmond.

To give me some time, Desmond tells Nana's favorite riddle: *"The rope runs, but the horse stands still.* What is it?"

Miss Tilly, the head cook, calls out the answer. "A yam vine growing up a pole!" Then she and her helpers hold out trays of roasted nut-flavored yellow yams and salt fish. I can't even look at the food.

Soon Maas Halroy says, "Sareen would like to tell us her stories of Nana."

My heart pounds. My throat feels as if I've swallowed a stone.

"You can do it," Desmond whispers.

Mama gives me an encouraging nod.

Looking at faces that outnumber the stars, I tremble. Everyone stares at me. I can't concentrate or remember. I have to close my eyes.

The traditional dress I'm wearing feels like Nana's embrace. She sewed it for my folk dance at the festival. Now memories of her flood my mind.

I say, "Nana used to tell me, 'If happiness has a taste, it's the taste of a ripe mango.' So when she got sick this mango season, I wanted to make her happy by giving her the sweetest mango I could find."

The silence makes me want to run away. I fight to catch my breath, and then I go on, "But mangoes were scarce this season. Our tree had only a few. One night I thought I heard the sound of a mango hitting the ground. I dashed out into the moonlight and scooped up something dark from under the tree.

"It felt soft. It squeaked. I screamed and dropped it. It was a bat!" People are laughing at me. Maas Halroy steadies me as my knees wobble. Then I realize that people are laughing at my bat story. I'd forgotten how funny many of my memories of Nana are.

I open my eyes and say, "The next morning Nana told me, 'It was a

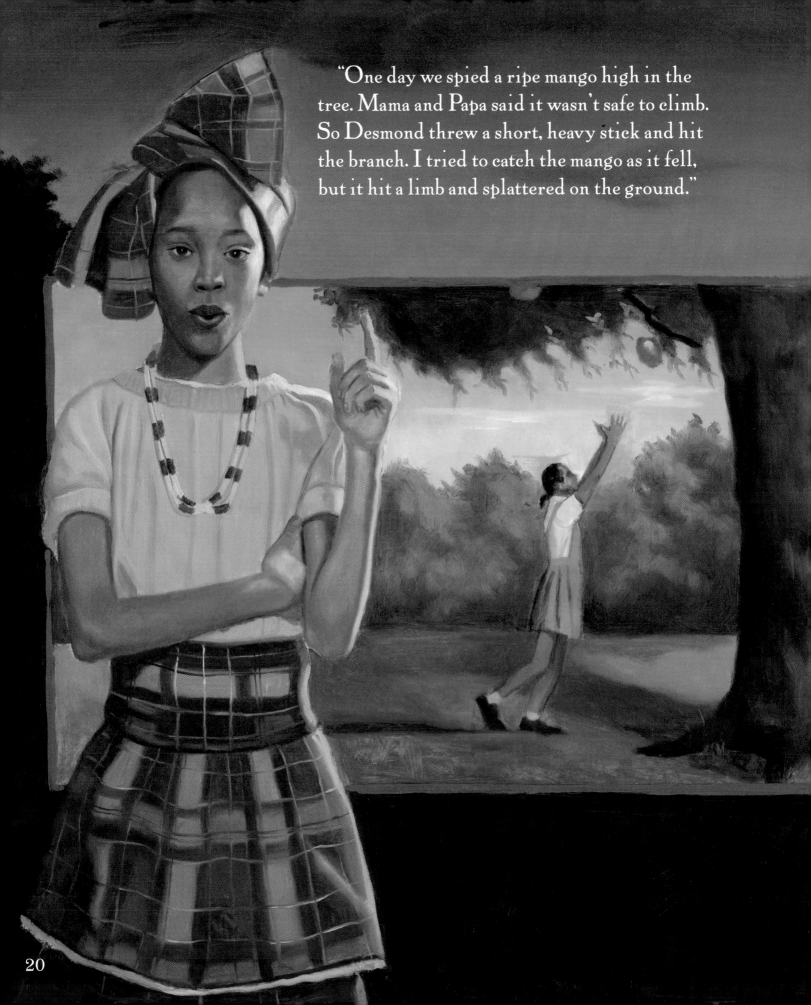

"One day we spied a ripe mango high in the tree. Mama and Papa said it wasn't safe to climb. So Desmond threw a short, heavy stick and hit the branch. I tried to catch the mango as it fell, but it hit a limb and splattered on the ground."

People groan, and I know they feel as disappointed as I did. This story seems to be telling itself. I say, "Desmond and I made a cushion around the tree with coconut limbs and dried banana leaves, so that if I missed catching another, the mango would have a softer landing.

"We didn't want Nana to see how upset we were about the ruined mango. So we got our baskets and went fishing for jang-ga.

"As Nana ate jang-ga soup for dinner, we told her all about the fishing. She said, 'It was a good day. You had an adventure in a mountain stream, and that gave me my favorite crayfish soup.'"

People smile and nod. They're really listening.

I say, "When Nana became very ill, we were sitting at her bedside, holding her hand and reading to her. And, and—"

I can't talk anymore. Tears stream down my face.

Papa brings me a kerchief and gives me a hug. Desmond holds a water coconut for me to sip.

I dry my eyes. In the many splashes of light I see others drying their tears. They loved Nana and miss her, too. That comforts me.

After a deep breath, I continue my story. "We were sitting with
Nana when we heard a mango fall onto the cushion of dry leaves.
It was ripe-ripe and the sweetest ever. When I fed the mango to Nana,
her eyes lit up. I told her, 'It's a wonderful day, Nana. You got the
perfect mango of the season—the taste of happiness.'"

The pleasure I felt at that moment rushes through me again now. I say, "This is what I'll remember best about Nana. Mangoes made her happy, but she was happy every day, even when she didn't get a mango."

My stories over, I curtsy.
"Well done!" Maas Halroy exclaims.
Desmond gives me a big grin.
Everyone stands, and the hills echo with
the clapping of the whole village.

I could burst with delight. Nana would
have been proud of me. I never guessed it
would feel so good to tell my memories of
her. Now they seem even sweeter than that
last mango.

Dawn peeks over the mountain tops.
Maas Halroy announces, "This is the most
important moment. We will jump the kooma
for Nana!"

27

Grownups form the great circle of life around the mango tree. Each holds a bamboo pole upright. They step to the beat of the drums. All together they strike the earth with the poles, as if to ask the ancestors to take good care of Nana, who is buried among them.

I take my place at the front of the circle of dancers. The drumbeat quickens. Chills race up my spine.

As the grownups continue their dance, I begin my own. It's as though telling my stories about Nana lifted away a lot of my sadness, making me lighter on my feet. With all my love, I dance to celebrate her.

Then I dance to thank everyone for this happy sit-up that is helping me say goodbye to her.

The drums beat even faster. I leap again and again. Raising my arm, I jump higher and higher to knock on heaven's door, so that it will open for Nana's spirit. I leap to make my heart dance, so that whenever it thinks of Nana, it will remember her joy.

AUTHOR'S NOTE

According to Jamaican folklore, a ghost returns from the grave for nine nights after death. Each night, it visits familiar places and collects the shadows of favorite possessions to take with it to the next world.

The lore says that on the ninth night, friends and family should hold a wake, or sit-up, to entertain and feed the ghost—called a *duppy*—so that it will leave happy and in peace. If the duppy isn't satisfied, it will keep coming back to trouble the living. The sit-up, also called a *nine-night*, should end before the last cock crows at dawn, for if the ghost isn't back in its grave by then, it becomes a roaming and mischievous duppy.

Some of Jamaica's wake customs arrived with slaves from West Africa beginning in the sixteenth century. Many slaves died from cruel treatment and overwork. Facing these losses, the survivors found comfort in their traditions, and endured.

The wake customs have changed over time and are less common today, but Jamaican children still love duppy stories. Sareen's family holds the sit-up not to observe beliefs from folklore but to honor Nana and affirm her life.

Along with West Africans, people from Great Britain, India, China, the Middle East, and other parts of the world helped to create Jamaica's unique culture. The nut-flavored yellow yam was introduced to Jamaica from West Africa and is one member of the family of true yams. Sweet Thanksgiving "yams" are actually varieties of the sweet potato. The practice of cooking a goat with curry seasonings came from India.

When I'm in Jamaica, I feast on scrumptious "East Indian" mangoes. My passion for mangoes, inherited from my grandmother, led to this story. During her sit-up, ripe mangoes kept falling from a nearby tree. A visitor joked, "Her duppy is picking mangoes for us!" Some lucky guests promptly enjoyed the fruit.

As a child growing up in Jamaica, I looked forward to mango season each summer, when I always listened for the sound of a mango hitting the ground. At night, the sound would awaken me. What happened to Sareen in the story really happened to me—I once was fooled by a bat in the moonlight!